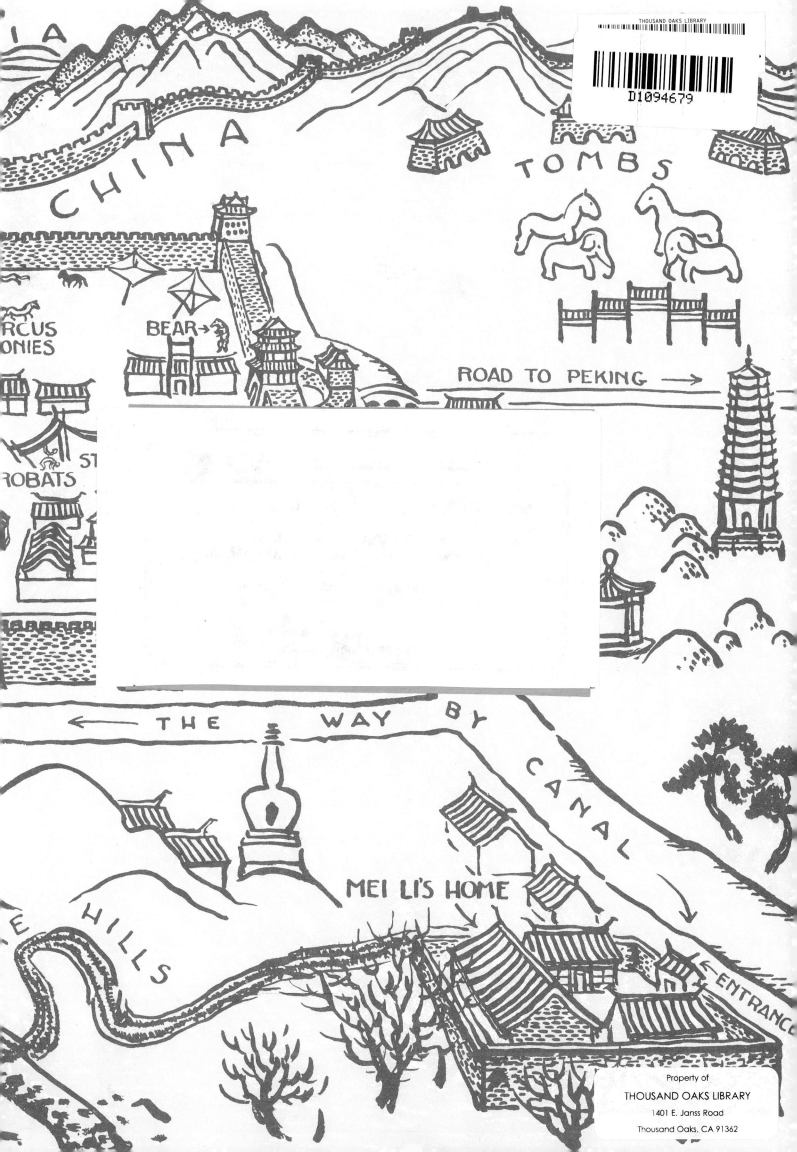

MEI LI

by
THOMAS HANDFORTH

如意　吉祥

DOUBLEDAY

NEW YORK　LONDON　TORONTO　SYDNEY　AUCKLAND

We keep a dog to watch the house,

A pig is useful, too,

We keep a cat to catch a mouse,

But what can we do

With a girl like you?

TRANSLATED FROM THE CHINESE
BY ISAAC VICTOR HEADLAND

MEI LI

In North China, near the Great Wall, is a city shut in by a Wall. Not far from the city in the snow-covered country is a house with a wall around it, too. Inside the house on the morning before New Year's Day, everyone was very busy. Mei Li, a little girl with a candle-top pigtail, was scrubbing and sweeping and dusting. Her mother, Mrs. Wang, was baking and frying and chopping. Her brother, San Yu, was fixing and tasting and mixing. A fine feast was being prepared for the Kitchen God, who would come at midnight to every family in China to tell them what they must do during the coming year.

Only Uncle Wang sat without working. He was talking and laughing and singing of the sights to be seen in the city. Often, with his camels, he went there to sell vegetables; so he knew.

San Yu stopped to listen happily, because his mother had just told him that he could go that day to the New Year Fair in the city.

Mrs. Wang stopped to listen cheerily because she thought of

the red candles and paper money that San Yu would bring back to please the Kitchen God.

Mei Li stopped to listen sadly because little girls always had to stay home.

"Eiya! Eiya!" she whimpered to herself, wagging her candle-top. "If I always stay at home, what can I be good for? I am going to take my lucky treasures and have adventures like San Yu."

Into the pocket of her winter big coat Mei Li packed her three lucky pennies and her three lucky marbles—one lapis blue, one coral red, and one jade green.

Then she followed San Yu little by little through the court-

yard, being careful to wish a happy New Year to the ducks and pigs.

"New rejoicing, Mrs. Ugly Pig!" she said, bowing politely.

"New rejoicing, Stupid Mr. Duck!" she said, again bowing politely.

When no one was looking she slipped quickly through the gate.

Outside the gate Mei Li caught up with San Yu.

"Please, San Yu, take me on the ice sled with you as far as the city gate," she whispered.

"What can a girl do at the Fair?" scoffed San Yu.

"I will give you my lapis-blue marble if you will," said Mei Li.

And San Yu whispered back, "Can-Do."

Then Igo, the small white dog, begged to go, too. San Yu's thrush did not want to be left at home either. So San Yu, Mei Li, Igo and the thrush all set out together on an ice sled. A man pulled it, slipping and sliding down the frozen canal.

They zipped and they whizzed along the snow-white canal.
Soon they came to the bridge just outside the city. There Mei Li
gave one of her lucky pennies to a hungry beggar girl.

"Thank you, thank you!" said the girl, whose name was Lidza.

"What fun for a girl to go to the Fair! A lucky penny will bring you luck. But remember! You must be back before the Big Gate closes, or you will not be able to leave the city and go home tonight. And then you could not greet the Kitchen God."

Across the bridge a donkey was waiting for them. San Yu, Mei Li, the thrush and Igo climbed on his back, and jerkity-jerk he trotted off through the gate in the thick wall.

Now they were inside the city, trotting along a wide street.

They saw people riding in rickshas, and people on camels, ladies in glass carriages, men on shaggy Mongol ponies, and other boys and girls on donkeys. And all of them were dressed in their finest clothes, and all of them were going merrily to enjoy the New Year holiday. It was just as exciting as Uncle Wang had said.

It was lunchtime when they arrived at the Great Square. There some of the city children were eating bean-curd sweets and buying sugared fruits on long sticks.

Mei Li wanted candy too, but even more she wanted a firecracker. She spent her second penny on firecrackers. She was too frightened to shoot them off herself, so she gave them to San Yu and ran away with her fingers in her ears.

"Bang! Bang!" popped the crackers.

"Pooh! Pooh!" sneered San Yu. "Girls are always afraid. What
can a girl do at the New Year Fair?"

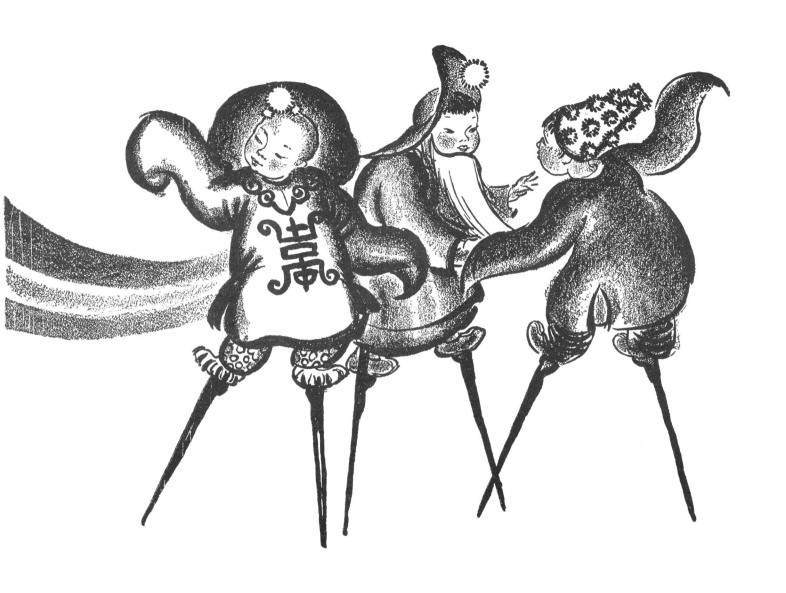

"Lots of things," said Mei Li. "Look at those girls in the circus over there. They can walk on stilts. They can balance on a tight-rope. They can throw pots and pans in the air with their feet. And so can I!"

She ran to a circus girl who looked strong. "Oh, please, will you hold me upside down in the palm of your hand?" Mei Li begged. "I want to try it."

The circus girl lifted her high in the air.

Mei Li balanced all right, but her legs wobbled a little.

"Ho!" jeered San Yu. "Anyone can learn that kind of trick. But only boys can be real actors!" San Yu had dressed himself up as a wise old man with a silly long beard. He was performing with one of the boys in the traveling show who was dressed like an emperor with a crown like a pot of flowers. They were singing songs together in high squeaky voices.

Girls couldn't be actors, Mei Li knew. She looked around for something else to do. There in one corner of the Fairgrounds,

was a black bear with a ring in his nose. She would show San Yu how brave she was. She would make the bear do tricks!

Mei Li's candle-top trembled as she held out a bit of bean-cake to the bear. The bear bounced up and down and flapped his padded paws, begging for the cake.

"That's a tottering, *tame* old bear," shouted San Yu. "Watch me while I hunt a wild, wicked lion!"

"Mercy!" squealed Mei Li. "That long-eared thing is not a lion, but two boys with a mask and a straw tail. Be careful not to shoot them!"

Mei Li ran now to join some girls who were riding circus
ponies. Her pony pranced around the ring, and her candle-top
bobbed up and down as she danced on his back. She was beginning

to feel like a real circus performer, but suddenly she missed San Yu.

She hurried down the street and found him at the Bridge of Wealth. Under the Bridge of Wealth hung a little bell, and

under the bell lay a skinny, wrinkled priest who mumbled, "Ring the bell with a penny, and you will have money for all the year."

"Oh," wailed Mei Li, "my last lucky penny, and the bell is so tiny! I'm sure I could never hit it. Here, San Yu, you throw it for me." And she gave her last penny to San Yu.

"Ting-ling!" tinkled the bell.

"Ho, I am rich!" sang San Yu. "Igo and I are going to buy a kite. Look after my thrush while I'm gone."

"Oh," spluttered Mei Li, and her candle-top whisked with

rage, "my last lucky penny! What can I do now?" She started sadly up a near-by hill. And there at the top, under a gnarly old pine tree, sat a smooth young priest telling fortunes with bamboo sticks.

"Tell me a fine fortune and I'll give you my coral-red marble," pleaded Mei Li. "My brother is going to be rich, and I want to be as lucky as he."

"You will rule over a kingdom," replied the priest, waving his magic wand over the sticks and taking the coral-red marble.

Mei Li ran happily down the hill. Surely, if the fortune sticks said she was going to rule a kingdom she would. But how could she rule a kingdom unless she was a princess? And who ever heard of a princess without a crown?

At the foot of the hill she met some girls who were all dressed

up to go to the Fair. Mei Li told them about the fortune and they helped her to make a crown with a jade-green marble fixed in front.

Mei Li's candle-top wagged proudly above it as she strutted down the street. This was much more fun than performing in a circus. She came to a large toy shop.

Surely a princess with a crown could visit a toy shop, even though she had no lucky pennies to spend, thought Mei Li. Inside there were rows upon rows of tiny figures, priests, peddlers, dancing girls, wise men, musicians, monkeys and deer.

"Perhaps," thought Mei Li, as she played, "they are all here to honor me!" But the little figures were made of painted wood, and very soon Mei Li left them.

The next room was bright with New Year lanterns made to

look like fishes. All the bulgy fishy eyes stared at her.

"They are looking at my lovely crown," thought Mei Li, and her candle-top swished with vanity.

In the next hall, large grasshopper, crab, turtle and moth lanterns stared at her. But the Princess Mei Li did not feel happy with such big, unpleasant bugs. She had never seen any like those in the walled garden at home. She hurried outdoors.

Outdoors a strong wind was blowing. Suddenly a gray hawk swooped through the cold sky. Mei Li pressed San Yu's thrush close to her, so that the hawk could not hurt it. She ran as quickly as she could toward the market place. The hawk swooped close, and closer, and closer still!

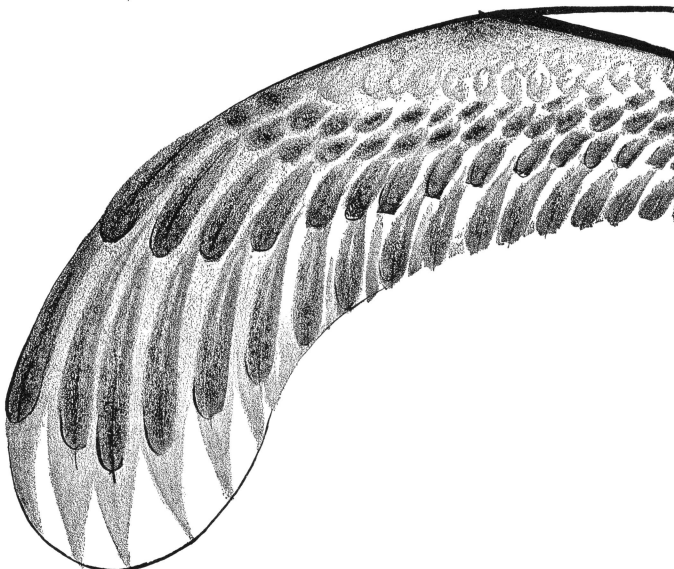

"Poor little thrush!" thought Mei Li, her candle-top stiff with fright. "What can I do to save you?"

Just then a large goose escaped from its basket. Quickly Mei Li crawled under the basket and lay still as dead.

Thump! Thump! Thump! beat her heart. "Haw! Haw! Haw!" echoed some throaty snorts.

"Those 'haws' are not hawk 'haws'," Mei Li said to her thrush. She peeked through a hole in the basket and saw three clumsy camels laughing at her.

"Ha! Ha! Ha!" came from the other side, and three deep voices said, "There's the rascal we're looking for!"

"Bandits!" thought Mei Li. Again she lay still as dead, and her heart beat Thump! Thump! Thump!

Then she felt a tug, tug, tugging at her candle-top and a tug, tug, tugging at her trousers, and a yap, yap, yapping in her ear and a yap, yap, yapping at her feet It was Igo.

"Tee-hee-hee!" hooted San Yu, who had been hiding behind a baby camel. "That wasn't a hawk chasing you, it was only my kite."

"You are brave for a girl, to protect San Yu's thrush, but don't you know your own uncle in his fur hat?" said Uncle Wang. "I have been hunting for you all day, and if we don't hurry back on the camels, before the city gate closes, we'll not get home tonight to greet the Kitchen God."

"Up we go," said Uncle Wang, and he climbed on the first camel, holding Mei Li safely in front of him. San Yu and his thrush sat on the second camel, and Igo rode proudly by himself on the third.

And then the camels, with the riders between their humps and the baby camel tagging behind, gallumphed through the evening light. Faster and faster they raced through the darkening streets: through the falling sparks of bursting New Year rockets. They were too late! The city gate was swinging closed!

But no! Lidza, the beggar girl, was holding the heavy door open with her feet. She knew that Mei Li must be home by midnight to greet the Kitchen God. And even five policemen and five soldiers could not force her away until Mei Li was through the gate.

Faster and faster the camels sped on and up and on and

down through the hills that looked like dragons in the dark night.

Mei Li's pennies were gone. Her marbles were gone. Her crown was lost. She was so hungry that her stomach ached, and so tired that her candle-top lay flat on her head. Prancing ponies, bouncing bears and long-eared lions seemed to be following her. She had forgotten she was a princess.

And surely no kingdom could be as nice as home. How glad she was at the sight of her house among the trees behind the wall!

"Oh, the best part of going to the Fair is getting home," cried Mei Li, as Uncle Wang lifted her down from the camel's back. "And we are still in time for the New Year feast."

"Do not be sad because you have brought home no presents," said Mrs. Wang to San Yu. "You have brought us the princess who rules our hearts." And while she waited to greet the Kitchen God, Mei Li wondered: "Even Mamma knows that I am a princess just as the fortune sticks said, but where can my kingdom be?"

At midnight, when the Kitchen God appeared behind the flame and smoke of burning incense, behind the honey cakes and dumplings which Mrs. Wang had cooked for him, he said solemnly, blinking at Mei Li, "This house is your kingdom and palace. Within its walls all living things are your loyal, loving subjects."

Mei Li sighed happily, "It will do for a while, anyway."

Published by Doubleday, a division of
Bantam Doubleday Dell Publishing Group, Inc.
666 Fifth Avenue, New York, New York 10103

Doubleday and the portrayal of an anchor
with a dolphin are trademarks of
Doubleday, a division of Bantam Doubleday Dell
Publishing Group, Inc.

Library of Congress Cataloging-in-Publication Data
Handforth, Thomas, 1897–1948.
Mei Li/by Thomas Handforth.
p.   cm.
Summary: After spending an eventful day at the fair held on
New Year's Eve, Mei Li arrives home just in time to greet
the Kitchen God.
[1. China—Fiction.]   I. Title.
PZ7.H192Me   1990
[E]—dc20   89-1456   CIP   AC

ISBN 0-385-07401-8 (trade)
ISBN 0-385-07639-8 (library)
RL: 3.0

This is the thrifty princess,
Whose house is always clean;
No dirt within her kingdom
Is ever to be seen.

Her food is fit
For a king to eat;
Her hair and clothes
Are always neat.